To Suz, who loves to mow the lawn
even more than I.

Typeset in Century Schoolbook.
The illustrations in this book are created by hand
and colored on the computer.
Manufactured in Hong Kong.

Library of Congress Cataloging-in-Publication Data
Frazier, Craig, 1955-
  Stanley mows the lawn / Craig Frazier.
     p. cm.
Summary: While mowing his lawn, Stanley meets Hank, a snake
who prefers the grass long.
  ISBN 0-8118-4846-9
  [1. Lawns–Fiction. 2. Snakes–Fiction. 3. Human-animal
  relationships–Fiction.] I. Title.
  PZ7.F869Stm 2005
  [E]–dc22
2004017017

Distributed in Canada by Raincoast Books
9050 Shaughnessy Street, Vancouver, British Columbia, V6P 6E5

10 9 8 7 6 5 4 3 2 1

Chronicle Books LLC
85 Second Street, San Francisco, California, 94105

www.chroniclekids.com

STANLEY

Mows the Lawn

Craig Frazier

chronicle books · san francisco

The grass in Stanley's yard had grown so tall that he couldn't even see the toes of his boots.

So Stanley started mowing his huge lawn. Up and back, up and back, up and back.

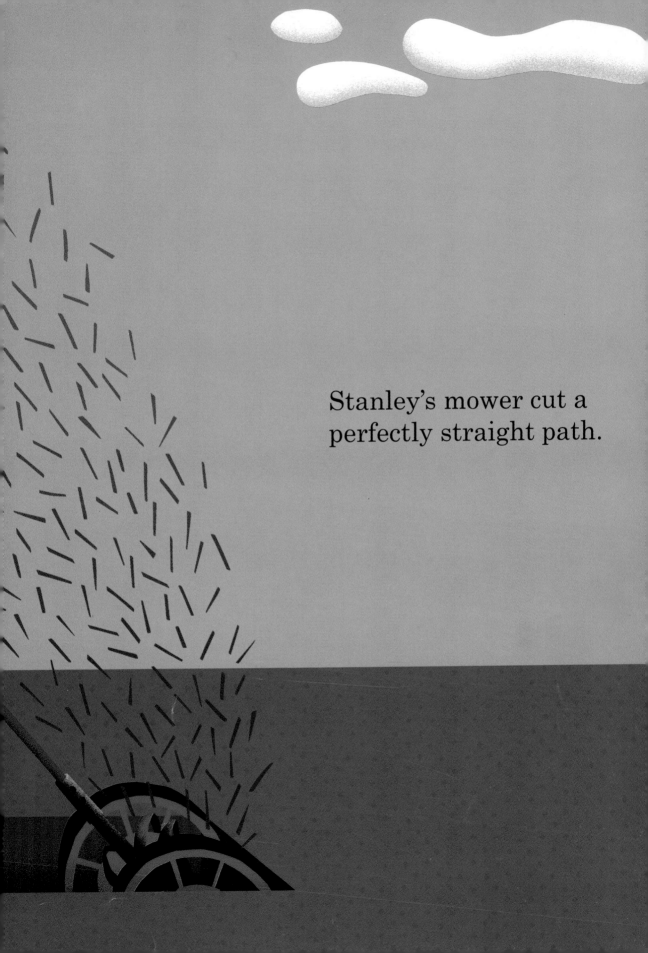

Stanley's mower cut a
perfectly straight path.

The grass clippings flew everywhere.

Suddenly, Stanley stopped mowing.
He heard something moving inside
the tall grass.

It was Hank the snake. Hank stopped
because he heard something moving
outside the tall grass.

Hank bravely poked his head out
so he could get a better look.

Stanley bravely knelt down so he could get a better look.

Then, right before Stanley's eyes, Hank slithered across the short grass and back into the tall grass.

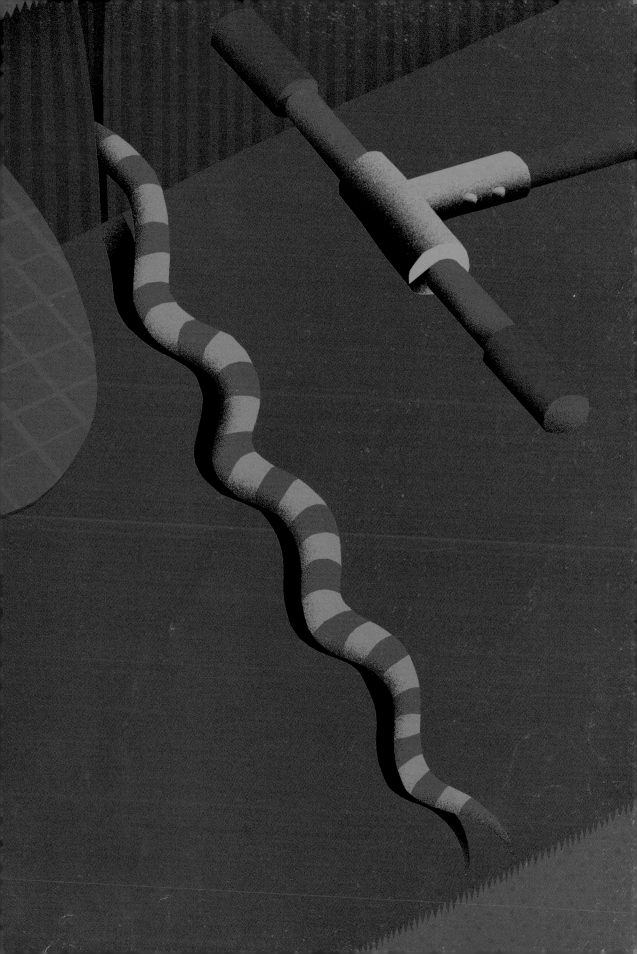

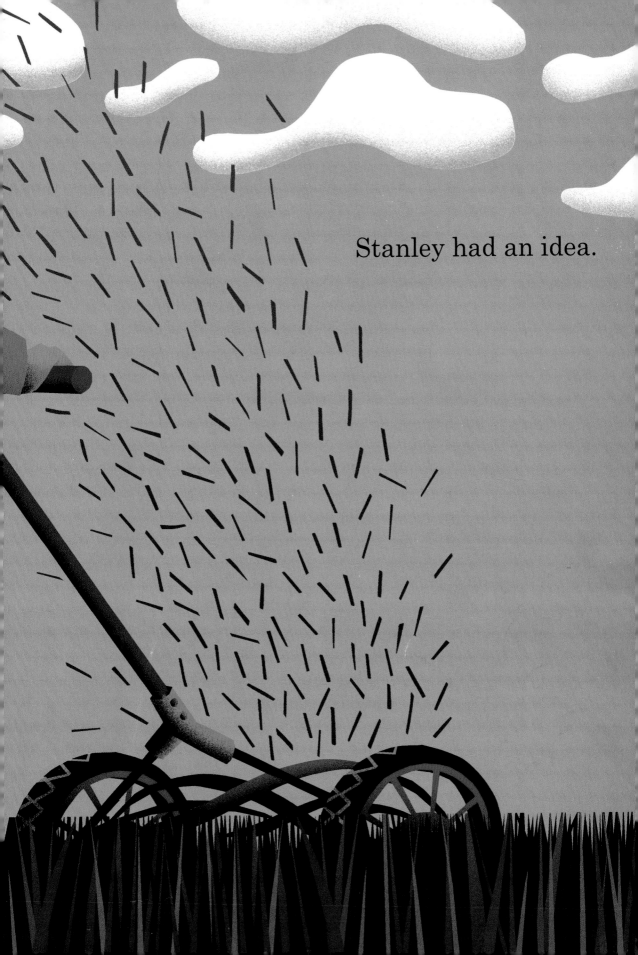

Stanley had an idea.

Stanley zigged.

And Stanley zagged.

When Stanley finished mowing,
he looked at his lawn. He liked it.

And so did Hank.

Sssssee you later.

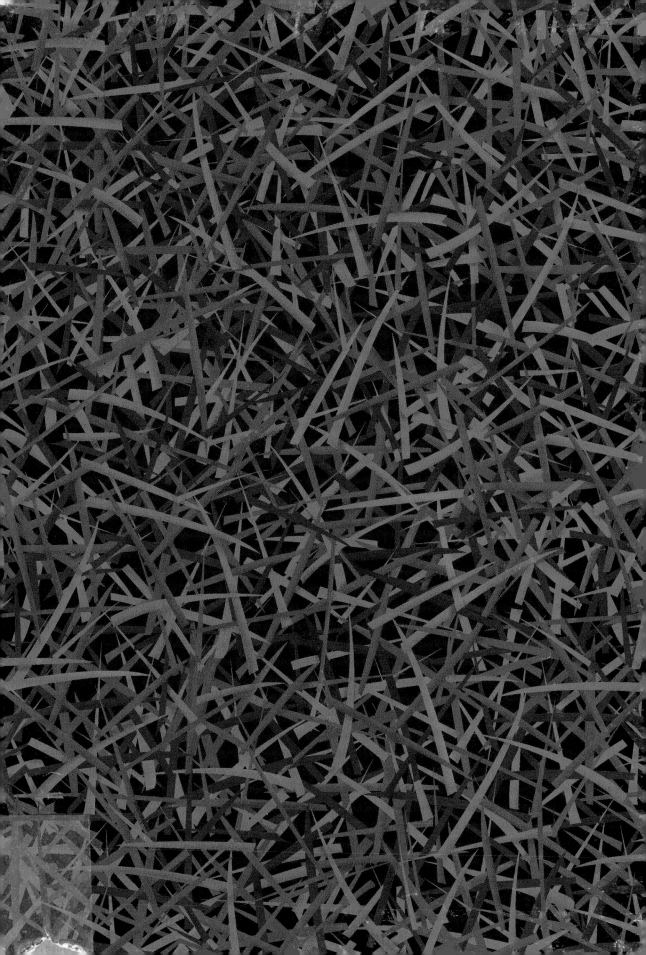